My "q" Sound Box®

WRITTEN BY JANE BELK MONCURE • ILLUSTRATED BY REBECCA THORNBURGH

The Child's World®
childsworld.com

Published by The Child's World®
1980 Lookout Drive • Mankato, MN 56003-1705
800-599-READ • www.childsworld.com

ISBN HARDCOVER: 9781503823204
ISBN PAPERBACK: 9781503831421
LCCN: 2017960381

Printed in the United States of America
PA02371

A NOTE TO PARENTS AND EDUCATORS:

Magic moon machines and five fat frogs are just a few of the fun things you can share with children by reading books with them. Reading aloud helps children in so many ways! It introduces them to new words, motivates them to develop their own reading skills, and expands their attention span and listening abilities. So it's important to find time each day to share a book or two . . . or three!

As you read with young children, you can help develop their understanding of how print works by talking about the parts of the book—the cover, the title, the illustrations, and the words that tell the story. As you read, use your finger to point to each word, modeling a gentle sweep from left to right.

Simple word games help develop important prereading skills, including an understanding of rhyme and alliteration (when words share the same beginning sound, such as "six" and "sand"). Try playing with words from a book you've just shared: "What other words start with the same sound as moon?" "Cat and hat, do those words rhyme?" The possibilities are endless—and so are the rewards!

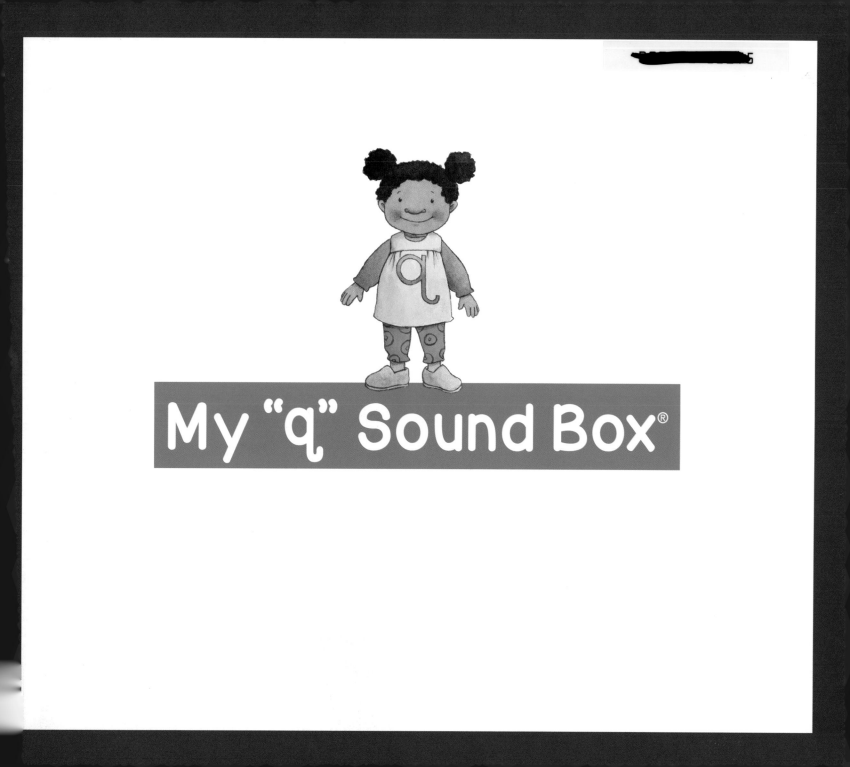

My "q" Sound Box®

Little 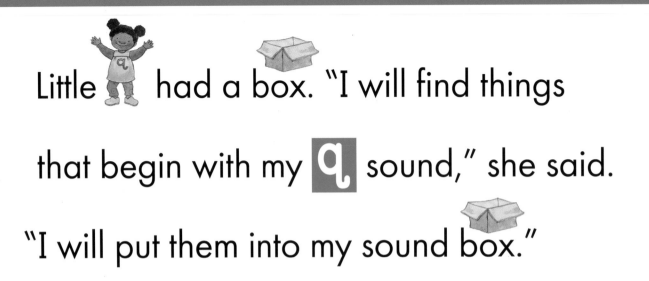 had a box. "I will find things that begin with my **q** sound," she said.

"I will put them into my sound box."

Little  found quilts. . .

. . . quite a lot of quilts! Two

quails watched her quietly.

Little  folded the quilts. She filled her box with quilts.

There was one quilt left. Little
wrapped the quilt around herself.

"I can be a  queen," she said.

Just then, Little  met a real  queen.

"If you want to look like a real queen,

you must have a crown," said the queen.

So Little  found some quarters. . .

quite a lot of quarters! She counted her

quarters. How many did she have?

Little  took the quarters to the store. Little

bought a crown. The two  queens played

until they were quite hungry.

Little  found a  quart of milk and some

quince. Then she and the  queen ate lunch.

Little  put what was left into the box.

Then Little  said, "It is late! It is time to go to bed."

"No, no," said the  queen. "A real  queen must have a  queen's bed."

Little  looked for more quarters so

that she could buy a  queen's bed.

She looked and looked. But she

could not find any more quarters.

Then Little a saw her box with all the quilts inside.

"I will turn my box into a 📦 queen's bed," she said.

Little  put a quilt on top of the box. "Now we can go to bed," she said. She jumped into the box.

"No! No! No!" said the real  queen.

They quarreled and quarreled

until quarter past nine.

Then the real queen was so

tired of quarreling

that she quit!

She got into the box with Little .

They pulled up the quilt and went to sleep.

Little 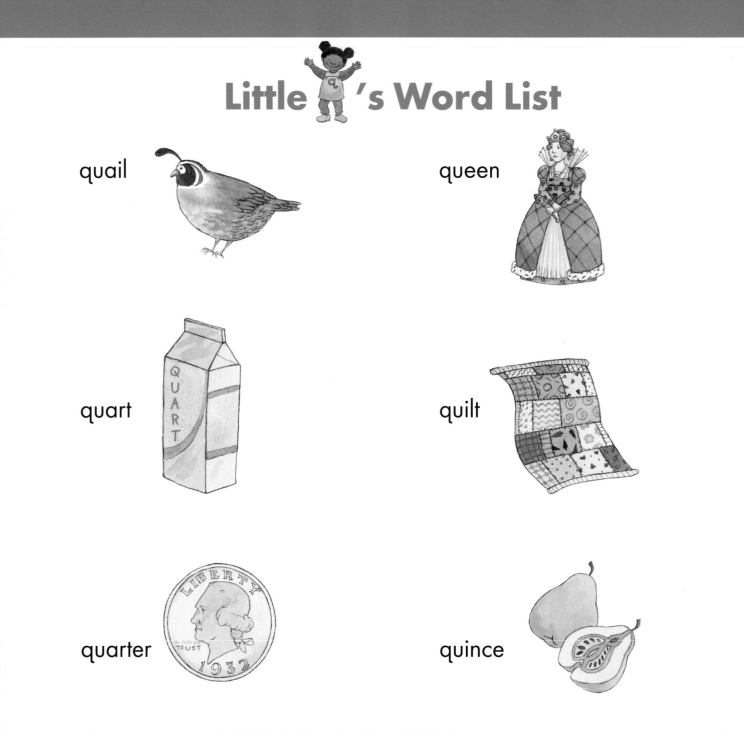's Word List

quail

queen

quart

quilt

quarter

quince

Other Words with Little

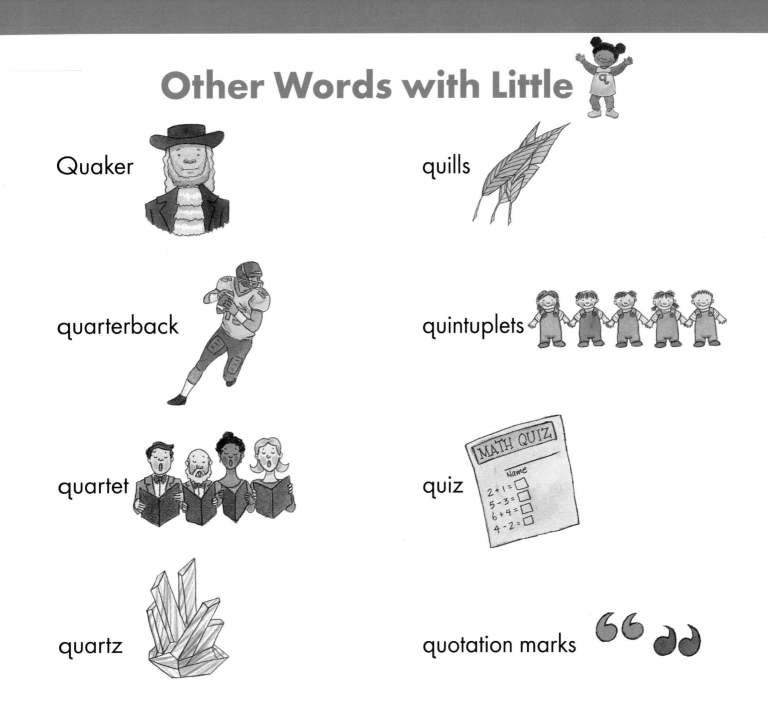

Quaker

quills

quarterback

quintuplets

quartet

quiz

quartz

quotation marks

About the Author

Best-selling author Jane Belk Moncure (1926–2013) wrote more than 300 books throughout her teaching and writing career. After earning a master's degree in early childhood education from Columbia University, she became one of the pioneers in that field. In 1956, she helped form the Virginia Association for Early Childhood Education, which established the first statewide standards for teachers of young children.

Inspired by her work in the classroom, Mrs. Moncure's books became standards in primary education, and her name was recognized across the country. Her success was reflected not only in her books' popularity with parents, children, and educators, but also by numerous awards, including the 1984 C. S. Lewis Gold Medal Award.

About the Illustrator

Rebecca Thornburgh lives in a pleasantly spooky old house in Philadelphia. If she's not at her drawing table, she's reading—or singing with her band, called Reckless Amateurs. Rebecca has one husband, two daughters, and two silly dogs.